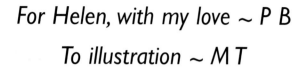

For Helen, with my love ~ P B
To illustration ~ M T

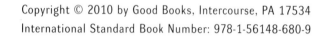

Copyright © 2010 by Good Books, Intercourse, PA 17534
International Standard Book Number: 978-1-56148-680-9

Library of Congress Catalog Card Number: 2009028294

Text copyright © Paul Bright 2009
Illustrations copyright © Michael Terry 2009
Original edition published in English by Little Tiger Press,
an imprint of Magi Publications, London, England, 2009
Printed in China

Library of Congress Cataloging-in-Publication Data

Bright, Paul.

Crunch munch dinosaur lunch! / Paul Bright ; [illustrations] Michael Terry.

p. cm.

Summary: Ty tyrannosaurus stomps through the jungle proving that he is brave,
terrifying, and hungry, while his loving baby sister, Teri, keeps embarrassing him,
but when she is threatened, Ty comes to the rescue.

ISBN 978-1-56148-680-9 (hardcover : alk. paper) [1. Brothers and
sisters--Fiction. 2. Tyrannosaurus rex--Fiction. 3. Dinosaurs--Fiction.]
I. Terry, Michael, ill. II. Title.

PZ7.B7649Cru 2010

[E]--dc22

2009028294

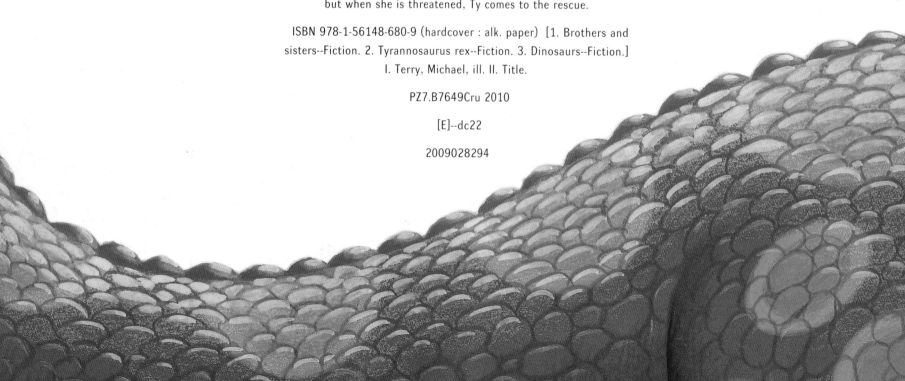

CRUNCH MUNCH
DINOSAUR LUNCH!

Paul Bright   Michael Terry

Good Books

Intercourse, PA 17534
800/762-7171
www.GoodBooks.com

Ty was big, and Ty was mean. He had a big, big mouth, with big, big jaws, and big, big teeth and big, big claws.

"Yeah! That's me," said Ty tyrannosaurus.

His roar echoed around the swamp
so that the other dinosaurs trembled
in their tummies.

ROAR!

Teri was small and Teri was sweet. She had a tiny, tiny mouth, with tiny, tiny jaws, and tiny, tiny teeth and tiny, tiny claws. And she loved her big brother more than any tyrannosaurus has ever been loved.

"Wuv oo, Ty rannynormus!"

gurgled Teri.

"Stay in your nest, pest," said Ty.

"I've got hunting to do."

Ty stomped through the swamp.
The ground sploshed and quaked and
quivered, and the dinosaurs heard
and shook and shivered.

"I'M HUNGRY!" roared Ty.

"I'M BIGGEST, I'M BADDEST, AND I'M READY TO EAT. I NEED SOME FRESH STEGOSAURUS MEAT!"

He opened his big, big mouth and . . .

"Hug oo, Ty rannynormus!"
burbled Teri, wrapping her
arms around his huge leg.

Ty sighed as he saw his stegosaurus breakfast
paddle off through the swamp, snickering.
"You shouldn't be here, squirt!" he hissed.
"Get back to your drooling. Now stay away!"
And off he stomped, snorting.

Ty searched in the swamp. The dinosaurs ran and hid. They peered through the reeds and peeked from behind rocks. But it's not easy to hide when you're a dinosaur.

"I'M STARVING!" roared Ty.

"I'M BIGGEST, I'M BADDEST,
AND I'M READY FOR LUNCH!
I NEED TRICERATOPS BONES
TO CRUNCH!"

He bared his big, big teeth and . . .

"Kiss oo, Ty rannynormus!" slobbered Teri, planting a wet, sloppy kiss on his huge cheek.

Ty moaned as he saw his triceratops lunch plodding through the trees, laughing.

"You crawling, bawling bug!" he growled. "Get back to your slurping and burping. Now leave me alone!" And off he stormed, snarling.

Ty crept through the swamp, quiet as quiet.
The other dinosaurs stayed still as still,
and even the leaves stopped rustling.
But a dinosaur can't stay still for long.
Ty heard a movement in the trees
and saw a long, long neck.

"I AM RAVENOUS!" roared Ty.
"I'M BIGGEST, I'M BADDEST,
AND I NEED A TREAT!
DIPLODOCUS STEAK LOOKS
TASTY TO EAT!"

He roared a big, big roar and . . .

"Cuggle oo, Ty rannynormus!"
cooed Teri.

Ty groaned as his
diplodocus steak waddled
into the reeds, chuckling.

"You spoiling, sniffling, dribbling,
burbling, gurgling pest!" he bellowed.
"I've had nothing to eat all
day because of you."

"GRRRR!
I'M GOING HOME!"

Ty stomped off through the swamp, then pounded across the plain in a great temper. Teri watched him getting further and further away. Then she sat down in a heap and howled.

THUD! THUD! THUD!

Suddenly . . . the ground trembled.

"Ty rannynormus!" squeaked Teri.

But it wasn't.

IT WAS SPINOSAURUS!

Teri screamed. Spinosaurus was huge—
bigger even than her big brother Ty.
He had a huge, huge mouth, with
huge, huge teeth, and his
mouth was opening
wider and wider!

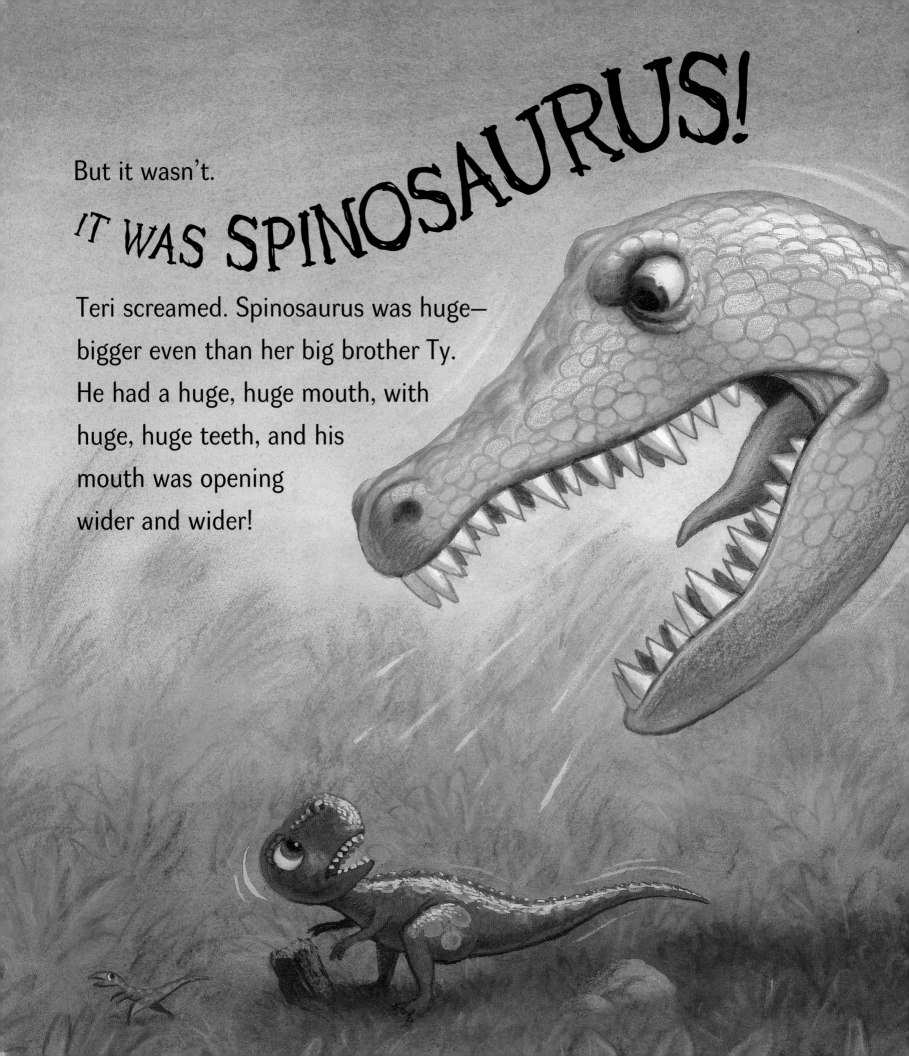

Ty roared and raged. He charged and chased.
And Spinosaurus turned and ran,
as fast as his lumbering
legs could go.

Then Ty reached down and scooped up Teri in his big, brotherly arms. He hugged his favorite, very annoying pest of a sister more tightly than any tyrannosaurus has ever been hugged.

"Wuv oo, Ty rannynormus,"

gurgled Teri.

"Wuv oo too, Teri rannynormus,"

said Ty, with a big, big smile.

"Now let's go get some dinner!"